P9-BJN-911

First edition 2022

Illustrations copyright © 2022 Ivan Tu
Book Design by Ashley Santoro

ivandaydreams.com

Follow Ivan
 @ivandaydreams

TABLE OF CONTENTS

Part 1: 5

1. Wander not wonder 7
2. A division in the mind 9
3. In Circles 11
4. Broken 13
5. Big Unscalable 15
6. The Purpose Circus 17
7. Tied Down 19
8. Stan the Stag 21
9. Repetition 23
10. Flip the switch! 25

Part 2: 27

11. Inner Demon 29
12. The Steps 31
13. Temptation 33
14. Ol'tub of I Scream 35
15. Bear with Me 37
16. Glued to you 39
17. Chasing a feeling 41
18. The One 43
19. King Do-Nothing 45
20. Apathy Island 47

Part 3: 49

21. Money Hog 51
22. Half-Full and Half-Empty 53
23. In Peril 55
24. Apart 57

25. Sparkles 59
26. Risk 61
27. Deep eyes 63
28. Mr. Eel 65
29. Faith and Fate 67
30. Wish U Well 69

Part 4: 71

31. University of Adversity 73
32. Easy vs Hard 75
33. Self Reflection 77
34. Hair 79
35. Meat 81
36. Set the bar 83
37. Keep Trying 85
38. Space 87
39. On a Roll 89
40. Daydream 91

Part 5: 93

41. Dino I know 95
42. Look Up 97
43. Duck 99
44. Kids 101
45. Music 103
46. Little Snooze 105
47. A tune 107
48. Beginning to end 109
49. Winning 111
50. Build your boat 113

Part 1:
Lost, where will you go?

Wander not wonder

Everyone wanders now and then
I wonder this. I wonder that.
This path here, this path there,
no map to show you where is where—
to be where you need to be,
you must wander, not wonder.
Only then will you see where you could be.

A division in the mind

A division in the mind—
split decisions bind you.
You gave your all to reach the top,
up on the fence and ready to drop.
One look down, one side to choose—
make one choice, there's nothing to lose.

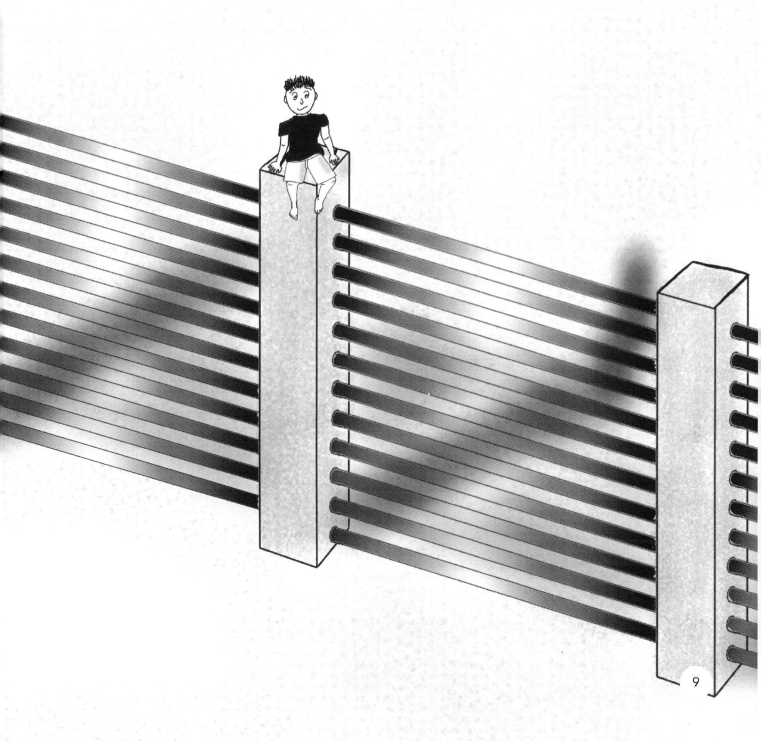

In Circles

I've had it with this addict.
Repeat and repeat is all I do.
"I need it now. I want it now.
I can't stop. I won't stop."
I want to stop going in circles.
Tell me: How do I draw the line?

Broken

Before I was broken good,
I was cheerful-eyed—
fellow with a mellow demeanor.
Then you unwrapped me,
exposed me after you used me
and left me a broken good.

Big Unscalable

Oh! Big, unscalable
wall so tall,
miles high in the sky—
please, let me up,
for I am weak and small,
not mighty at all,
and though I may fall,
I will climb
and climb
and climb
until I am unable.

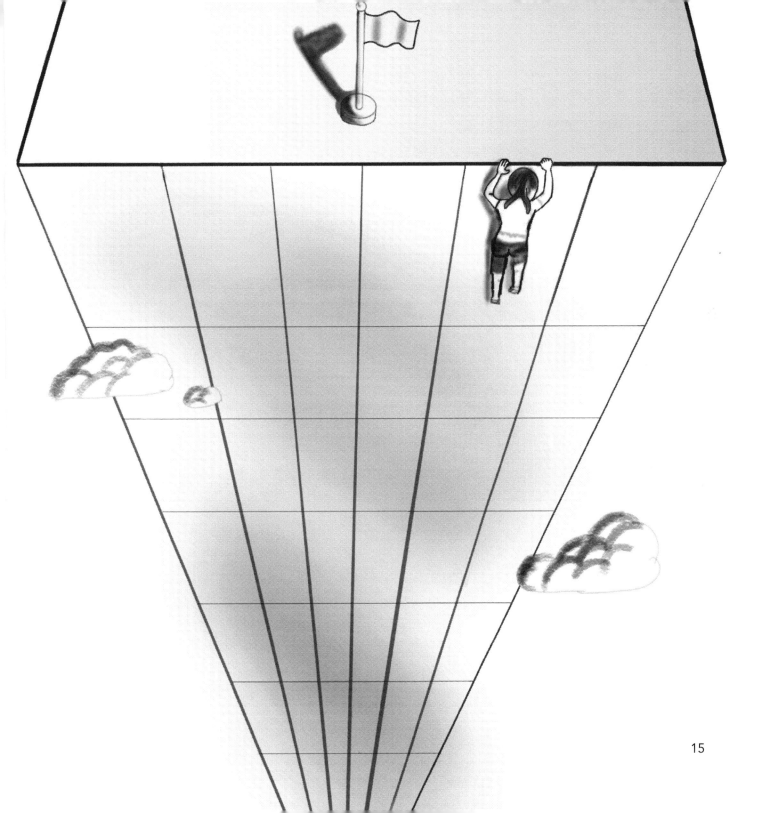

The Purpose Circus

Come one, come all!
Welcome to the Purpose Circus,
where your greatest dreams might come true:
juggling, tumbling, and all the ladders you can climb!
Do you live for fun and games?
Well, come on in—come now!
You're in for a show!

17

Tied Down

You can't take flight if you're tied down.
Open skies are off-limits
when you're Earth-bound.

You could soar to new heights.
You were born with wings.
Something holds you back—heavier than gravity.
Too many chicks?
Never left the nest?
Too late for the early worm?
Your life's a mess?

Stressed?

Your quest is yet to fly!
In the end, only you choose your fate:
Stay tied down?
Or fly free!

19

Stan the Stag

Stan the Stagnant Stag refuses to start anew,
but he sure can make the quick buck.
To the past, he cannot say, "Adieu."
Sure, it would behoove his hooves to move,
yet still. he chooses to remain.

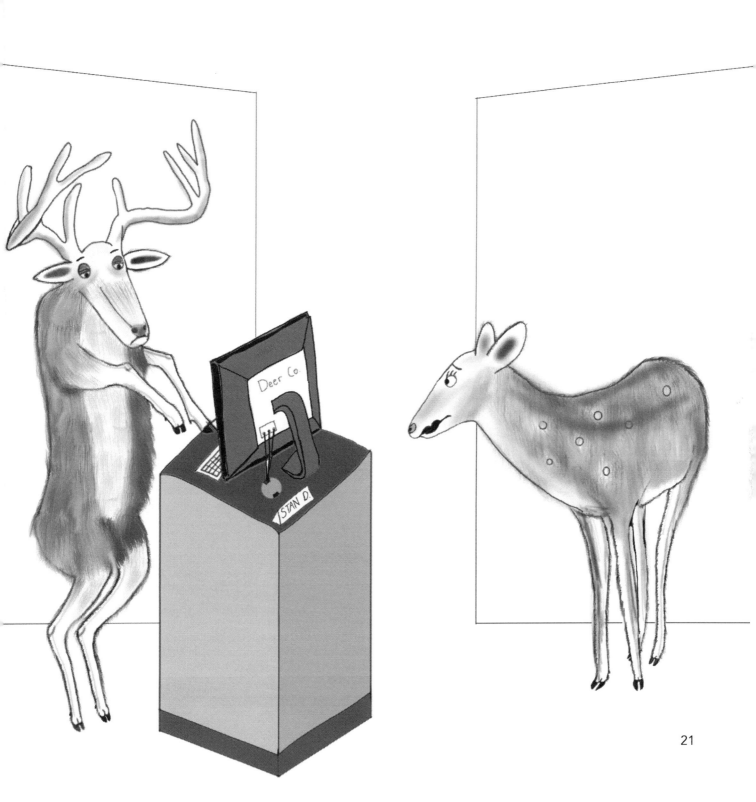

Repetition

Repetition is attrition:
it wears you down over time.
Repetition is a war against the mind:
two sides that can't make do.
Repetition's a foolproof trap:
you can escape any time—but can you?
Repetition is this poem,
telling you to try new things.

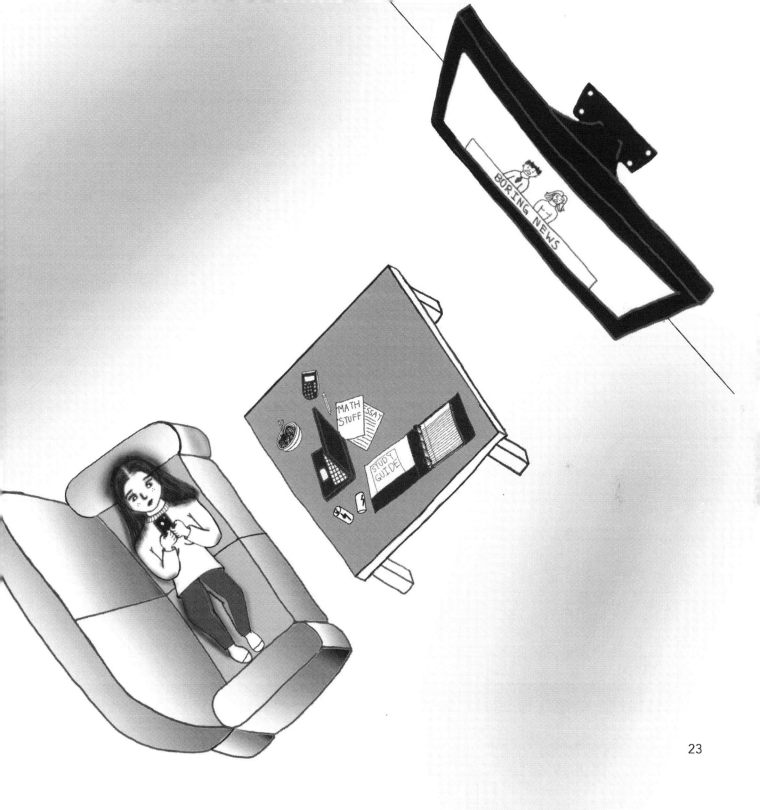

Flip the switch!

A switch in my head is off—
little guy in there took a snooze,
called it quits 'cause he's had enough.
No wonder my brain's so hard to use.
Wake up now! Flip the switch!

Part 2:
Face your demons.

Inner Demon

I'm bottled up inside:
not a good place to hide.
You won't set me free.
You're afraid of what you'll see.
I'm your guilt.
I destroy what you've built.
I can't be reasoned with.
I'm your inner demon.

The Steps

Take it step by step.
Don't wait. Don't wait!

Temptation

Temptation punctures the soul,
like a needle pierces a balloon.
Slowly but surely, I lose myself.

Upon first waking, I find the gate is sealed—
flood of thoughts damned, 'til soon,
my mind drowns in temptation.

One gaze into the abyss, monsters unveiled—

day falls, revealing the fleeting light
and emptiness.

Running aimlessly, you'd think my head is full of air
stuck to a man's body, but I assure you,
I'm just readying a dive out of sight and away
from the devil's wicked harpoon.

Ol'tub of I Scream

When I lose my mind,
get myself in a bind—
just need to unwind
with a big ol' tub of I scream.

Big ol' tub
of
I scream

Bear with Me

Just bear with me please,
for I am more than teeth and claws.
I can be quite friendly, so be at ease—
from my fuzzy ears to my gentle paws—
once we clear the air,
you'll see there's more beneath bear fur

—unless I eat you.

Glued to you

I'm glued to you—
can't peel me off you.
I've got your back,
even if you push me back.
I'm attracted to you
so do you love me too?

Chasing a feeling

I'm chasing a feeling that swings on a string,
just out of reach. "What an annoying little thing,"
I think. Great lengths taken,
obstacles overcome—methodical,
comical, 'cause it slips between
my clinging fingers—just a little fling and, a sinking feeling.

The One

When you keep trying to
win "the one,"
you might just end up
getting none!

King Do-Nothing

In the Kingdom of Boredom,
there is a slight problem
that troubles the King of Do-Nothing,
a task so menial and small.
We've waited nearly four falls—
for him to just get up and Do-Something!

Apathy Island

On Apathy Island,
all is whatever.
Stress or worry?
There is never—
nothing to share,
no one to care.
Stony faces are at hand.
Are you sure you want to stay with us
—on this land?

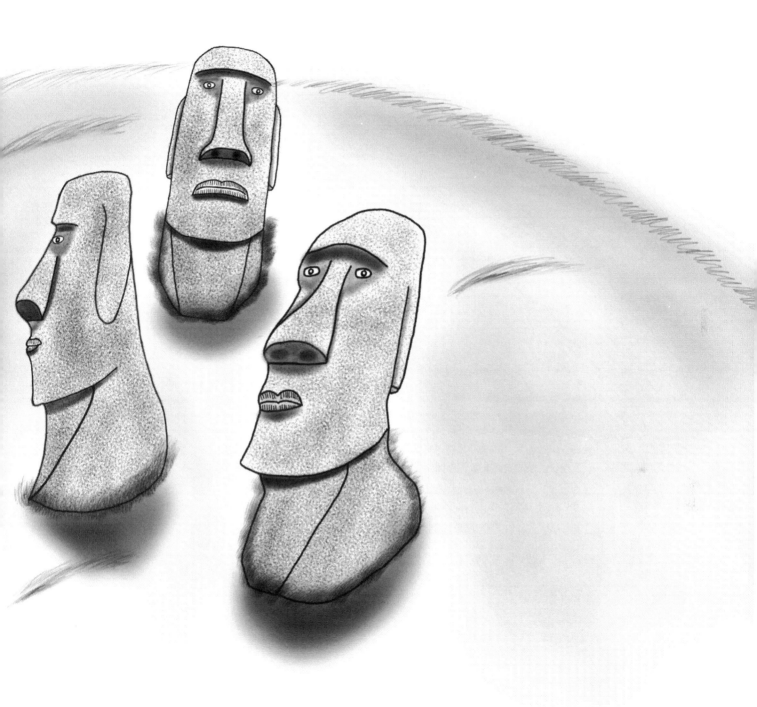

Part 3:
Change your Mindset.

Money Hog

The money hog is a greedy pig,
for atop his pile, from which he never shares,
he oinks of his riches and feels rather big.
Worry not!
This pig will someday realize no one cares.

Half-Full and Half-Empty

Half-Full and Half-Empty:
one and the same, both think alike—
a fulfilling life is their means to an end.
In one regard, though, they are quite
unlike: one is almost there,
the other not past halfway.

To give Half-Empty a chance,
Half-Full decided to share.

Now Half-Empty is Half-Full
because someone chose to care.

In Peril

I find paradise in peril,
though others may oppose.
I fair well when I'm feral.
I love to dance with danger,
when my life hangs by a thread.
I still live to win the divine wager.
I thrive on the pleasure of a thrill,
so don't blow me off balance,
or surely I may perish in peril.

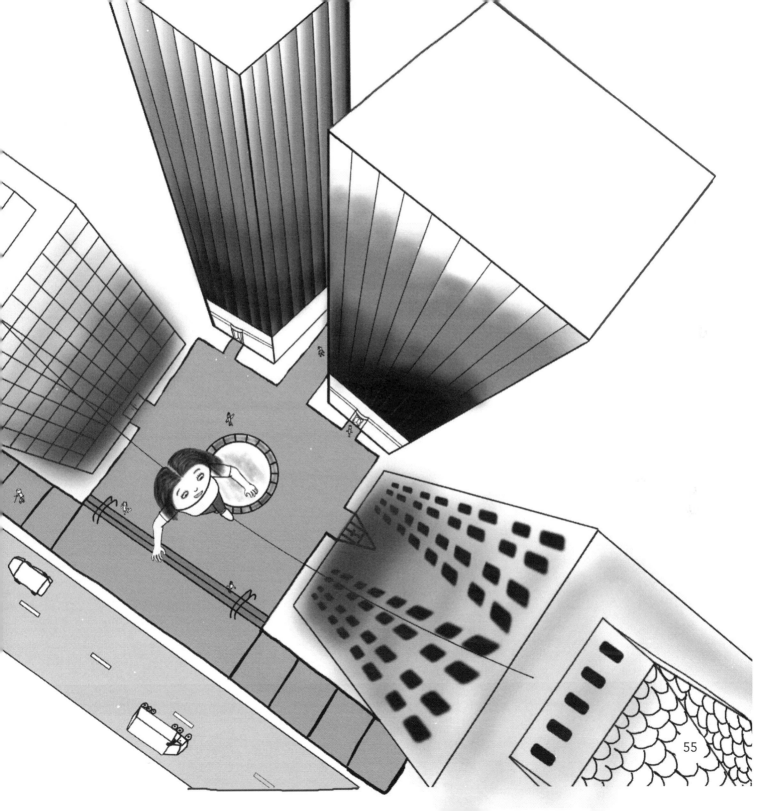

55

Apart

Once we had each other's backs.
Now our backs are turned to each other—
within an earshot, yet miles away,
although distance may do us part.
I'm a part of you now,
even when I'm apart from you.

Sparkles

When the sparkles die down,
silence in the air,
will you still be there?
When the colors go gray,
starry night laid bare,
will you still care?
When all is said and done,
and you no longer have any fun,
will we still be a pair?

Risk

"Calculated risk"
is a slippery slope.

Deep eyes

When I dive into your eyes,
I see what you can't disguise.
A whirlpool of feelings has you duped,
and now you've thrown ME for a loop.
Oh, but how I'm mesmerized
'cause I can't get enough of those eyes!

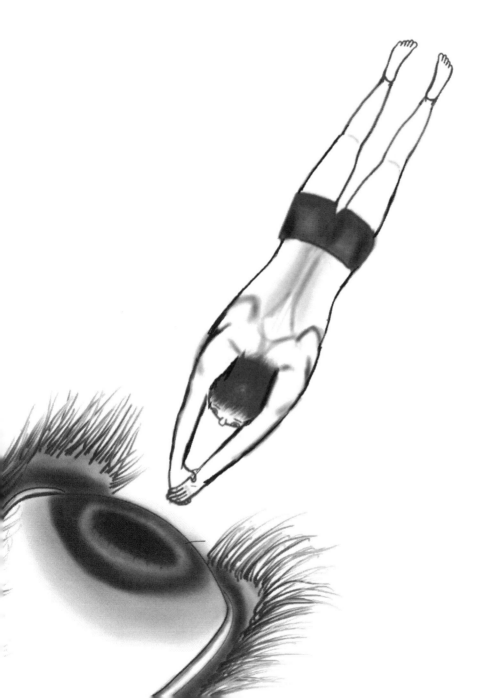

Mr. Eel

Mr, Eel cannot feel. He slips a lie and slithers about
into your heart and right back out.
Mr. Eel is a slippery fella.
To him you are nothing but a snack,
for he swims around with all the fish in the sea.

Faith and Fate

Your leap of faith,
daunting as it may seem,
is a fate you can't escape.
Shall you deem the feat too extreme?
Just hang tight and play it safe.
But the plane doesn't fly forever,
so please don't be the last one left.

Wish U Well

Oh wishing well, wishing well,
you're not looking so well!
I've given a wish too many.
Good and bad ones—there were plenty.
Then again, I didn't think a wish could sell.

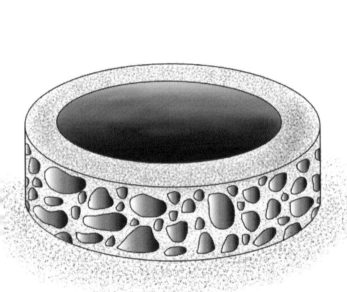

Part 4:

Almost There.

University of Adversity

The University of Adversity
is where misfortunes come to pass,
and bad things stay in the past.
New student, meet Professor Prudent,
master of caution and doing things right:
she's here to teach you the art of plight.
So wake from your naps.
Go put on your thinking caps,
you naughty little chaps.

Easy vs Hard

Try hard when you take it easy.
Take it easy when you try hard.

Self Reflection

A self-reflection of your reflection
exposes false impressions.
Look beyond what you see,
and you'll make a great first impression.

Hair

Would you like your hair—
shorter, darker, or slightly longer?
Here's a spray of water.
Don't make this any harder.
If you think you're smarter,
why'd you choose this barber?

Meat

If you are what you eat,
and all you eat is meat—
then you'll be dead meat.
So eat your veggies.
or I'll give you a wedgie!

Set the bar

Please lift my spirits.
I know I set the bar high,
and to shoulder this weight,
I'll need more than muscle.
So lend me the courage
to push all this weight on top.

Keep Trying

You are a failure.
Stop thinking that
You can finish what you started.
We believe.
You give up too easily.
Please don't.
Keep trying.

Read lines bottom to top now

Space

We're in trouble
if we start running out of space
in space.

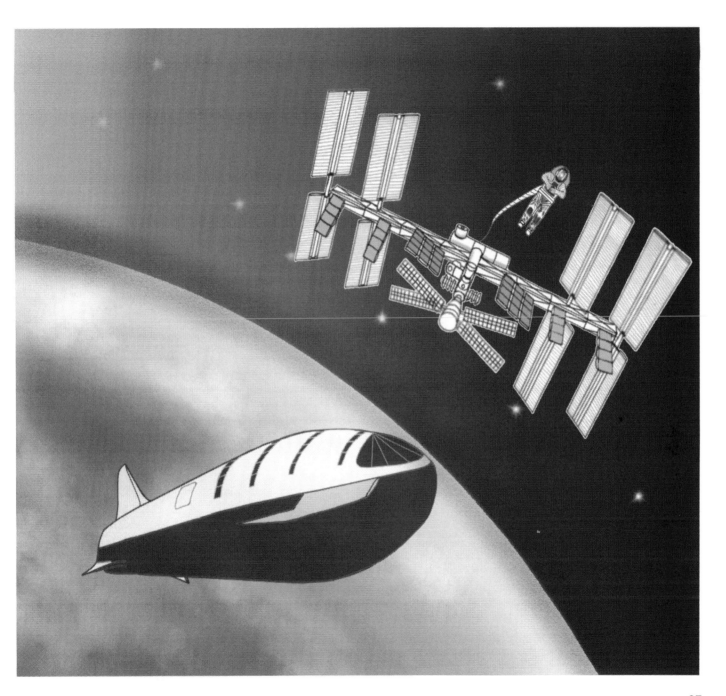

On a Roll

When you're on a roll,
you can coast right through
the ups and downs.

Daydream

A daydream a day
keeps the downs away.

Part 5 :
You found a direction!

Dino I know

There's a Dino I know
on the corner of Jurassic Row.

He's prehistoric, I think,
and frequently sick.

Sometimes when he falls down,
he can't get off the ground.

That's why I always go
to help the Dino I know.

Look Up

When your luck runs dry,
look up at the sky.
Don't ask why.

Duck

It's a pleasant day to be a duck,
floating near the docks.
A week of waddling to work—
awful!
It's nice to relax and paddle.
Uh oh! Here comes a boy,
who's looking rather coy.
If he tries to make a splash,
We better dash—
Quack! Quack!

Kids

Watch out! watch out!
There are kids playing about!
Moving back and forth,
it's fun to swing around!

Pitter patter,
our feet trample and pound!
Behold the chaos—
kids at a playground!

Music

Lose it to the music,
enter into trance,
and let your mind
dance.

Little Snooze

Gary had a little snooze,
little snooze, little snooze
Gary had a little snooze
He needs to get more sleep.

A tune

Can I sing you a tune
that I wrote on the fly?

It's okay if we're shy.
cause we can hold hands tomorrow noon.
I hope I'm not asking too soon,
but I couldn't let time pass by.

Now, before I say goodbye,
shall we give this thing a try?

Beginning to end

"Goodbye, I will miss you,"
she said to them at the beginning of the end.

"Hello, I've missed you,"
he said to her at the start of a new beginning.

Winning

A loop around the hoop—
good ol' twenty-four
can help you shoot your shot.
She passes the ball—
a layup on the way up.
Yes! The winning point!

Build your boat

Look to the future, and what do you see?
Infinite possibilities across the open sea?
Then go take a boat and stay afloat,
and when treasure finds you,
please leave a note!

Made in the USA
Coppell, TX
16 February 2022

73611463R00067